MARY POPPINS
AND THE HOUSE NEXT DOOR

Mary Poppins
and the
House Next Door

P. L. TRAVERS

with illustrations by
MARY SHEPARD

Delacorte Press

Published by
Delacorte Press
Bantam Doubleday Dell Publishing Group, Inc.
666 Fifth Avenue
New York, New York 10103

This work was first published in England by William Collins Sons & Co. Ltd.

The trademark Delacorte Press® is registered in the U.S. Patent and
Trademark Office.

Library of Congress Cataloging in Publication Data

Travers, P. L. (Pamela L.), 1906–
    Mary Poppins and the house next door.

    Summary: Luti, whom the formidable Miss Andrew has taken from
the South Seas to London in order to civilize, feels the need to go
home again, so Mary Poppins helps him get back to his island by way of
the Man-in-the-Moon.
    [1. Fantasy] I. Shepard, Mary, 1909–   ill.
II. Title.
PZ7.T689Mard   1989   [Fic]   89-1520
ISBN 0-385-29749-1

Manufactured in the United States of America

July 1989

10 9 8 7 6 5 4 3 2 1

BG

The *Mary Poppins* stories are written by a woman who welcomes, yet truly reveres, the power of Dionysus in the world. I say this partly out of gratitude, since my own appreciation of comedy, and of life, is derived in large part from *Mary Poppins* and partly because these stories include and illustrate two key aspects of "Dionysian fairy tale". The first is that with Mary Poppins, a wonderful transforming energy breaks through into ordinary custom and routine (which nonetheless remain extremely important) into a world of magic where the laws of nature are suspended. Part of the fun consists, naturally, of recognising familiar things in such strange and wonderful surroundings. Still more comes through surprise, incongruity and reversal. The fantasies are rich and fulfilling. They abound in delighted laughter and release. But they are also (and this is their second key aspect) ressuring, ultimately safe. Daemonic energies sometimes get loose, and they are very dangerous, but they are always brought back under control by the protecting figure of Mary Poppins, who is surrounded by the magic and excitement that she helps generate, but never really altered or affected by it. She always guides the children home again, back to safe and known reality – though some piece of the other world can still be glimpsed and its associated memories enjoyed. The world has been transformed a little, and we with it. That is why we can laugh so richly and well after reading and rereading these stories.

Aristophanes' Old-and-New Comedy
KENNETH J. RECKFORD (Professor of Classics at the University of North Carolina)

To Bruno

MARY POPPINS
AND THE HOUSE NEXT DOOR

Crack! went the teacup against the bowl of soapsuds. Mrs Brill, washing the china, scrabbled among the sparkling bubbles and fished it up in two pieces.

"Ah well," she said, as she tried, and failed, to fit them together. "It's needed somewhere else, I suppose." And she flung the two halves, with their twined roses and forget-me-nots, into the dustbin.

"Where?" demanded Michael. "Where will it be needed?" Who would need a broken cup? he wondered. It seemed a silly idea.

11

"How should I know?" fussed Mrs Brill. "It's an old saying, that's all. Now, you get along with your bit of work, and sit yourself down while you do it so that nothing else gets broken."

Michael settled himself on the floor and took the dishes as she handed them to him, drying them with the tea-towel and sighing as he did so.

Ellen had one of her dreadful colds, Robertson Ay was asleep on the lawn and Mrs Banks was taking an afternoon rest on the sofa in the drawing-room.

"As usual," Mrs Brill had complained, "no one to give me a helping hand."

"Michael will," Mary Poppins had said, seizing a tea-towel and thrusting it at him. "And the rest of us will go shopping and bring home the groceries. That will help."

"Why me?" Michael had grumbled, kicking a chair leg. He would like to have kicked Mary Poppins but that he would never have dared. For fetching the groceries was a special treat because, whenever the bill was paid, the grocer gave each of them – even Mary Poppins – a tasty liquorice stick.

"Well, why *not* you?" said Mary Poppins, giving him one of her fierce blue looks. "Jane did it last time. And somebody has to help Mrs Brill."

He knew there was no answer to that. If he mentioned liquorice, he would only get a short, sharp sniff. And anyway, even the King, he supposed, had sometimes to dry a dish or two.

So he kicked another leg of the chair, watching Mary Poppins as, with Jane carrying a string bag and the Twins and Annabel huddled into the perambulator, she went away down the garden path.

"Don't polish them. We haven't time for that. Just dry them and put them in a pile," Mrs Brill advised him.

So there he sat by the heaped up dishes, forced into doing a kindly act and not feeling kind at all.

And after a time – it seemed like years to Michael – they all came back, laughing and shouting and, sure enough, sucking liquorice sticks. Jane gave him one, hot from her hand.

"The grocer sent it specially to you. And somebody's lost the tin of cocoa."

"Somebody?" Mary Poppins said, tartly. "You, Jane, were carrying the bag! Who else could that somebody be?"

"Well, perhaps it just dropped out in the Park. I could go and look for it, Mary Poppins."

"Not now. What's done is done. Somebody loses, somebody finds. Besides, it's time for tea."

And she gathered the little ones out of the perambulator and hurried them all up the stairs before her.

In no time they were sitting round the nursery table waiting for hot buttered toast and cake. Except for the liquorice sticks, everything was the same as usual. Mary Poppins' parrot-headed umbrella, her hat, which today had a pink rose in it, her gloves and her handbag were neatly in their places. The children were all neatly in theirs. And Mary Poppins was going about her afternoon's work like a neat and orderly whirlwind.

"It's just like any other day," said Number Seventeen to itself, as it listened to the familiar sounds and felt the familiar movements.

But Number Seventeen was wrong, for at that moment the doorbell rang, and Mrs Brill came bustling into the drawing-room with a yellow envelope in her hand.

"Telelgram!" she announced excitedly to Mrs Banks. "Your Aunt Flossie's broken her leg, maybe, or it could be something even worse. I don't trust telegrams."

Mrs Banks took it with a trembling hand. She didn't trust telegrams either. They always seemed to bring bad news.

She turned the envelope over and over.

"Well, aren't you going to open it?" Mrs Brill was eager to know the worst.

"Oh, I don't think I will," said Mrs Banks. "I'd rather wait until my husband comes home. It is addressed to him, anyway. See – 'George Banks, Seventeen Cherry Tree Lane'."

"Well, if it's urgent, you'll be sorry you waited. A telegram is everyone's business."

Mrs Brill reluctantly left the room. She would

16

have enjoyed hearing bad news.

Mrs Banks eyed the yellow envelope, as it stood there on the mantelpiece, leaning against a photograph and coolly keeping its secret.

"Perhaps," she said hopefully to herself, "it's good news, after all. Mrs Brill doesn't know everything."

But she couldn't help wishing that this might be one of the days when Mr Banks came home early.

And, as it happened, it was.

He had got off the bus at the end of the Lane and was sauntering home past Number Twenty-One – Admiral Boom's house that was built like a ship – past Twenty with its honeysuckle hedge, past Nineteen with the fish pond in the garden, until he came to Number Eighteen.

And there he stopped, full of surprise, and not altogether pleased. Around the gate his neighbours were gathered, all talking earnestly together. The Admiral and Mrs Boom, Mr Twenty and Mrs Nineteen and Miss Lark from Number Sixteen. There was nothing odd in this, of course, a gathering of friends.

17

But what stopped Mr Banks in his tracks was the sight of a red-and-white striped tent, the kind that is put over open drains and other holes in the road. And beside it stood a brawny workman deep in conversation with the little group of neighbours.

"Ah, there you are, Banks, ship ahoy!" The Admiral's loud voice hailed him. "You're just the one to find out what this fellow thinks he's doing."

"I don't think, I know," said the workman, mildly. "I'm looking over this here house to see what repairs it needs."

"But it's empty," Mr Banks said, quickly. "it's been empty for years and years."

"Well, it won't be empty for long," said the man. "There's tenants coming in."

"But that's impossible," Mr Banks was distressed. "We all like it just as it is. Every street should have its deserted house."

"What for?"

"Well," began Mr Banks, a trifle uneasily, "so that people can fill it with their own ideas, the kind of neighbours they would like to have.

18

We don't want just anyone, you know."

There was a murmur of assent from them all as they thought of the long-empty rooms of their dear Number Eighteen.

For the Admiral they were inhabited by a sea captain who had sailed with Nelson and was ready at any moment, no matter what the weather, to heave up the anchor and put to sea.

Mrs Boom saw it as the home of a little girl with straight brown hair, the kind of child she would like to have had, who wandered about it, soft as a moth, humming gently to herself.

Mr Twenty, whose wife would never play chess with him, had friends there who were human chessmen – black and white kings and queens, bishops marching from corner to corner, knights riding up and down the stairs.

Mrs Nineteen, who was rather romantic, believed that in the empty house lived the grandmother she had never seen, telling wonderful bedtime stories, knitting pretty garments for her and always wearing silver slippers, even in the morning.

For Miss Lark, from Number Sixteen – the

grandest dwelling in the Lane – it was the home of another dog exactly like Andrew, an aristocratic little dog who would never choose, as Andrew had done, a vulgar friend like Willoughby.

As for Mr Banks, he liked to think that in the attic of Number Eighteen, lived an old wise man with a very special telescope which, when you looked through its round glass eye, could show you what the universe was up to.

"Anyway," he said to the workman, "it's probably not fit to live in after being empty for so long. Have you examined the drains?"

"All of them in perfect condition."

"Well, the chimneys. Full of starlings' nests, I'll be bound."

"Clean as a whistle," said the man.

"What about the furniture? Mice making tunnels in the beds. Cockroaches in the kitchen."

"Not a mouse. Not a 'roach."

"And the dust. It must be everywhere, inches thick."

"Whoever comes into this house," said the

man, "won't even need a duster. Everything's as good as new. And anyway," he began to dismantle his red-and-white tent, "houses are for human beings, not harum-scarum fancies."

"Well, if it must be, it must be," sighed Miss Lark. "Come Andrew, come Willoughby, we will go home." And she walked away dejectedly, the two dogs at her heels looking equally depressed.

"You should have gone to sea," said the Admiral, looking ferociously at the workman.

"Why?"

"A sailor would stay on the deck of his ship and not come making trouble for those who live on the land."

"Can't bear the sea, it makes me seasick. And anyway, it's no fault of mine. I have me orders, 'to be carried out forthwith', I was told. The tenants are coming in tomorrow."

"Tomorrow!" everyone exclaimed. This was terrible.

"Let us go home," coaxed Mrs Boom. "Binnacle is making curry for supper. You'll like that, won't you, dear?"

Binnacle was a retired pirate who daily kept everything ship-shape in Admiral Boom's ship-shaped house.

"Well, heave up the anchor and sail away, shipmates. There's nothing else to do."

The Admiral took Mrs Boom's arm and slouched off along the Lane, followed by Mrs Nineteen and Mr Twenty, both looking forlorn.

"A queer lot you are, I must say." The workman gathered up tent and tools. "All this to-do over an empty house!"

"You don't understand," said Mr Banks. "For us, it's not empty, far from it." And he turned towards his home.

Across the Lane, he could hear the Park Keeper doing his rounds. "Observe the Rules. Remember the Bye-laws." The starling on the top of Number Seventeen's chimney was giving his usual starling shriek. Laughter and shouting came from the nursery mingled with the comments of Mary Poppins. He could hear Ellen's endless sneezing, the clatter of dishes in the kitchen, the sleepy snores of Robertson Ay – all the familiar sounds of home, everything the same as usual, comfortable, intimate.

But now, he thought, everything would be different.

"I have news for you," he said, glumly, as Mrs Banks met him at the door.

"And I have news for *you*," she said. "There's a telegram on the mantelpiece."

He took the yellow envelope, ripped it open, read the message and was suddenly very still.

"Well, don't just stand there, George! Say something! Has anything happened to Aunt Flossie?" Mrs Banks was anxious.

"It is not Aunt Flossie. Aunt Flossie doesn't send telegrams. I will read it to you:
Coming to live at Number Eighteen.
Arriving 4.30 tomorrow. Bringing Luti.
No help required."

Mr Banks paused for a moment. "It is signed," he said, "Euphemia Andrew."

Mrs Banks gave a little shriek.

"Miss Andrew! Oh, I can't believe it. Our dear Number Eighteen!"

For Mrs Banks, too, had a friend in the house, a lady very much like herself who, when Mrs

24

Brill took long days off to see her cousin's niece's baby or Ellen had one of her fearful colds or Robertson Ay fell asleep in the rosebed, would throw up her arms when she heard the news and say, "Oh, how dreadful! How will you manage?"

This Mrs Banks found a great comfort. Now she must face her troubles alone.

"And Luti!" she cried. "Who could that be?"

"Probably not who but what. One of her medicines, perhaps."

Mr Banks sat down on a chair and put his head in his hands. Miss Andrew had been his governess when he was a little boy, a lady who, though strong as a camel, took medicines by the dozen; a lady so strict, so stern, so forbidding that everyone knew her as the Holy Terror. And now, she, of all people, was coming to live next door to him in a house that was full of his dreams.

He looked at the telegram. "No help required. Well, that's a blessing. I won't have to light a fire in her bedroom as I did that time she came to stay and disappeared so suddenly and went off to the South Seas."

"I wish she had stayed there," said Mrs Banks. "But come, dear, we must tell the children."

"I wish I were in the South Seas myself. Anywhere but here."

"Now George, don't be gloomy!"

"Why not? If a man can't be gloomy in his own house, where can he be gloomy, I'd like to know?" Mr Banks sighed heavily as he followed his wife up the front stairs looking like a man whose familiar world has fallen in pieces around him.

The nursery was in an uproar. Annabel was banging her spoon on the table, John and Barbara, the twins, were trying to push each other off their chairs, Jane and Michael were wrangling over the last piece of toast.

"Is this a nursery or a cageful of monkeys?" Mary Poppins was asking in her sternest voice.

"A cageful of . . ." Michael was about to be daring when the door suddenly opened.

"We have news for you all," said Mrs Banks. "A telegram has come."

"Who from?" demanded Jane.

"Miss Andrew. You remember Miss Andrew?"

"The Holy Terror!" shouted Michael.

"Hush! We must always be polite. She is coming to live at Number Eighteen."

"Oh, no!" protested both the children. For they did indeed remember Miss Andrew, and how she had once come to stay and had disappeared so strangely.

"But it's ours!" cried Michael. "Number Eighteen belongs to us. She can't come and live there!" He was almost in tears.

"I'm afraid she can," said Mrs Banks. "Tomorrow. Bringing someone or something whose name is Luti. And," she added coaxingly, "we must all be polite and kind, mustn't we? Mary Poppins, you'll see that they are neat and tidy and ready to greet her, won't you?" She turned timidly to Mary Poppins who was standing as still as a doorpost. It would have been impossible to tell what she was thinking.

"And when," she said acidly, looking as haughty as a duchess, "were they anything but

27

neat and tidy?" The idea was quite absurd.

"Oh, never, never," fluttered Mrs Banks, feeling as she always did with Mary Poppins as though she were a very small girl instead of the mother of five children. "But you know how fussy Miss Andrew is! George!" She turned anxiously to her husband. "Don't you want to say something?"

"No," said Mr Banks, fiercely. "I don't want to say *anything*."

And Mrs Banks, having delivered the unfortunate news, took her husband's hand and led him away.

"But I've got a friend who lives there," said Michael. "Gobbo, the clown we saw at the circus, who makes everybody laugh and looks so sad himself."

"I think the Sleeping Beauty's there, lying under a lacy quilt with a spot of blood on her finger." Jane, too, had her dreams of the house.

"She can't be," Michael protested. "There's no wall of thorns around it."

"There's nettles. They are just as good.

Mary Poppins!" Jane turned to the motionless figure, "Who do *you* think lives in Number Eighteen?"

Mary Poppins sniffed. "Five, nice, quiet, well-behaved children – not like some people I could mention."

Her blue eyes were sternly blue but in their depths was the glint of a twinkle.

"Well, if they're so perfect they don't need a Mary Poppins. It's we who need you," Michael teased her. "Perhaps you'll make *us* perfect."

"Humph," she retorted. "That's not very likely."

"Everyone needs her." Jane patted her hand, hoping to tease her into a smile.

"Humph," said Mary Poppins again. But the smile appeared as she met her reflection in the glass. Of course, each seemed to be telling the other, everyone needed Mary Poppins. How could it be otherwise?

Then the two mirrored faces resumed their sternness.

"Now, no more argle-bargling. Spit-spot

29

and into bed with you!"

And, for once, without argle-bargling, they did as they were told.

Much had happened. They needed to think it over, and were glad when their cheeks met the softness of their pillows, glad of the comforting warmth of the blankets.

Michael was thinking of Gobbo, Jane of the Sleeping Beauty. Their shadowy shapes would disappear from Number Eighteen and the solid figure of Miss Andrew would haunt the house instead.

"I wonder," said Jane, thoughtfully, "exactly what a Luti is?" She had never heard the word before.

"Perhaps it's an animal," said Michael. "Maybe a kangaroo."

"Or a monkey – a Luti monkey. I would like that," said Jane.

And they fell asleep dreaming of a kangaroo, or perhaps a monkey, gambolling happily about the Lane among the Cherry Trees.

But it was neither a kangaroo, nor a monkey, as they were to learn next day.

It was Saturday. Number Eighteen looked naked and a little lonely without its surrounding hedge of nettles. A workman had come in the early hours, cut them down and carted them off.

The Banks family spent a nervous morning, and as the afternoon drew on, Mr Banks, like an anxious general, marshalled his troops at the front gate.

"We must be there to greet her," he said. "One has to be polite."

"Don't keep fussing, dear," said Mrs Banks. "Perhaps she won't stay long."

Jane and Michael looked at each other remembering how, on her last visit, Miss Andrew had come and gone so quickly, and the part Mary Poppins had played in that curious departure.

They glanced at her as she stood beside them, rocking the Twins and Annabel in the perambulator, her face rosy and serene. What was she thinking? They would never know.

"There she is!" cried Mr Banks, as a hansom cab, hung about with Gladstone bags, turned from the main road into the Lane. "She

31

always travels with mountains of luggage. Goodness knows what is in it."

They all watched, holding their breaths, as the cabhorse wearily clopped along, dragging its heavy load – past Miss Lark's house, past the little group anxiously waiting outside Number Seventeen.

"Whoa, there," said the cabman, tugging at the reins, and the curious conveyance came to a stop at the gate of the empty house. He clambered down from his high seat and removed several Gladstone bags that hung from the roof of the cab. Then he opened the door and hauled out a large black leather trunk.

"Carefully, please, there are breakables in it," cried a haughty, familiar voice from within. A black-booted foot appeared on the step, then slowly, the rest of Miss Andrew, a large, ungainly, cumbersome figure, lumbered out onto the pavement.

She glanced around, and spied the family group.

"Well, George, I am glad you have not forgotten your manners. I expected you to meet me."

"Welcome, Miss Andrew!" Mr and Mrs Banks were rigidly polite.

"And the children seem clean and tidy enough. I hope their behaviour matches their appearance."

Then Miss Andrew craned her head and at the sight of the neat blue-coated figure standing in the background, she shrank back nervously.

"I see," she said, her voice trembling on the words, "that you still have the same young person taking charge of your household. Well, all I can say is, I hope she gives satisfaction."

"She does indeed," said Mr Banks, with a bow towards the blue coat.

"Welcome, Miss Andrew," said Mary Poppins, in a voice Jane and Michael had never heard, sweet, shy and unassuming. Miss Andrew turned her head away and her glance swept over the garden.

"Really, George, you live in a wilderness. Everything needs pruning. And what is that heap of garments doing in the middle of the lawn?"

"That," Mr Banks said, "is Robertson Ay.

He is taking a little rest."

"In the afternoon? Ridiculous! I hope you will take very good care that he never rests in *my* garden. Here," she turned, fumbling in her bag, to the heavily breathing cabman, "take the key and carry my luggage into the house."

"Well, I've just got to lever this here trunk." The man edged a chest through the door of the cab. "And then we can let out the little feller."

Jane and Michael looked at each other. Little feller! Did he mean a monkey or a kangaroo?

The chest fell with a thump on the pavement. It was followed by neither kangaroo, nor monkey, but by a small, strangely dressed boy, a little taller, perhaps, than Jane, with a large black bag in his hand. As he bent under the weight of it, they could see a round honey-coloured face with black hair falling loosely about it above a stiff white collar.

"Good Heavens!" said Mr Banks, in a whisper. "He's wearing my old clothes! She must have kept them all these years!"

The small figure, in knickerbockers, jacket and large brown boots stepped delicately down the step and stood there, hanging his head.

"This is Luti," pronounced Miss Andrew. "His name means Son of the Sun. He has come with me from the South Sea islands to get a good solid education and also to take care of me. Put down the medicine bag, Luti, and greet our next door neighbours."

The bag was put down, the bent head lifted. And as he beheld the group at the gate a smile lit up the sunburnt face as the boy took a step towards it.

"Peace and blessings," he said shyly, spreading out his arms.

"That will do," said Miss Andrew, sharply. "We don't use the island language here. Good afternoon is enough."

"And peace and blessings to *you*, Luti," Mr Banks cried heartily. "We are very glad to welcome you. There's a hole in the fence, just there," he pointed. "You can come through it at any time. My children will be delighted to see you – won't you, Jane and Michael?"

"Oh, yes!" said Jane and Michael, raptly. This was better than a kangaroo or monkey. It was a new friend to play with.

"George!" Miss Andrew's voice was like the snap of a whip. "Pray do not meddle in my affairs. Luti is here to work, not play. He will be busy with his lessons and making the porridge – we shall live on porridge, it is very nourishing – and getting my medicines ready. I intend him to be a credit to me so that when he eventually returns to the island he will go as something useful – a doctor or perhaps a teacher. In the meantime, we will continue our studies. And for relaxation, once a month, he and I *together*, George, will pay you a little visit. So go and waken your man, please, and tell him to repair the hole in the fence. We will have no to-ings and fro-ings between us. Is all the luggage safely in?"

She turned to the breathless cabman and gave him a coin as he nodded.

"Then pick up the medicine bag, Luti. We will go and inspect our new home."

She strode towards Number Eighteen and Luti, after a glance at Jane and Michael – they could not tell if it were sad or happy – shouldered his burden and followed her and the front door closed behind them.

The children looked at Mary Poppins. Her face was the only cheerful one among them. But now her smile was mysterious as though she was sharing a secret with herself.

"We will go in to tea," she said briskly, giving the perambulator a push, "and then perhaps a game of Ludo."

Jane and Michael enjoyed playing Ludo. But today it had no interest for them. They had something else on their minds. They followed slowly, dragging their feet, thinking of the golden boy who had appeared for a brief moment and then had been taken away.

"That poor child!" murmured Mrs Banks, looking tearfully at her husband.

"Well I said she was a Holy Terror." Mr Banks sighed deeply as he turned to the jumbled heap on the lawn to waken the sleeping figure.

And all the inhabitants of the Lane who had been leaning over their gates watching, went quietly into their houses. Number Eighteen was no longer theirs. There was nothing more to be said.

The Lane was silent except for the voice of the Park Keeper, "Observe the Rules. Remember the Bye-laws." And nearer at hand, the sleepy yawns of Robertson Ay as he put a nail to the loose paling and gave it a blow with his hammer. That done, he slid down on to the grass and went to sleep again.

Presently, the nail fell out, the paling gave a sideways lurch, and the hole in the fence between the houses was as it had always been.

Early next morning, when the sun rose over the trees of the Park, the Lane was peacefully asleep, not even a bird stirred.

Even so, something stirred. Jane and Michael, one carrying a banana and the other an apple, were tiptoeing cautiously through the nursery of Number Seventeen, past the camp bed where Mary Poppins lay sleeping, as neat and uncrumpled as though she and the bed were objects in a shop window. They smiled triumphantly at each other – Mary Poppins would not notice them! But at that moment, she

opened her eyes and her blue gaze fell upon them.

"And what do you two think you're doing?" She glanced at the fruit in their hands.

They jumped. She had woken, after all. "Well, Mary Poppins," Michael spluttered. "How would *you* like to eat nothing but porridge?" He eyed her anxiously.

"We thought, Mary Poppins," Jane tried to explain. "We thought if we put some food down by the fence, Luti . . ." she nodded towards Number Eighteen, ". . . might perhaps come and find it." She was as anxious as Michael.

Mary Poppins said nothing. She merely rose from her bed like a statue, leaving not a crease behind. Her hair hung in a plait down her back and her nightgown fell in neat folds around her as she stretched out her arm towards the door.

"Fetch me my handbag. It's hanging on the handle."

They ran eagerly to obey her and presently, sifting through the pockets, she took out of it a bar of chocolate and silently held it out. Michael made a rush at her and hugged her round the waist. He could feel her bony shape in his arms and her plait swung round his ears.

"Don't huggle and squeeze me like that, Michael Banks. I am not a Teddy Bear!"

"No, you're not," he cried, delightedly. "You're better than a Teddy Bear."

"Anyone can have a Teddy Bear. But we have you, Mary Poppins" said Jane.

"Oh, indeed?" she said with an uppish sniff, as she loosened Michael's hold. "Well, there's having and having, I assure you! Now go downstairs quietly, please, you don't want to disturb the household." And she pushed them before her to the door and closed it softly behind them.

Sleep was all about them as they crept through the house, slid down the banisters and tiptoed out into the garden.

No sound came from Number Eighteen as they placed the fruit and the bar of chocolate on the crossbar of the fence.

And no sound came from it all the morning as they played among the trees and flowers until Mary Poppins called them to lunch. Even when they raced down again, the banana, the apple and the chocolate were still in the same position.

But then, as they turned away from the hole in the fence, a strange noise came from the house next door – a deep and rhythmic rumble that went on and on and on. Everyone in the Lane could hear it and the house seemed to tremble with it.

The lady in Number Nineteen, who was of a nervous disposition, was afraid it might be the beginning of a volcano. Mr Twenty gave it as his opinion that it was a lion snoring.

Jane and Michael, watching from the branches of the pear tree in their back garden, felt that whatever it was, it must surely mean that something was going to happen.

And it did.

The front door of Number Eighteen opened and through it came a small figure, cautiously glancing from side to side. Slowly, he made his way round the house till he came to the hole in the fence, and then, seeing the fruit and the chocolate, he touched them with a delicate finger.

"They're for you!" shouted Jane, hurriedly scrambling down from her branch with Michael at her heels.

Luti looked up, a broad smile making his face like the sun, and he spread out his arms towards them.

"Peace and blessings!" he shyly whispered, cocking his head to one side, as he listened to the rumble.

"Missanda sleeps in the afternoon from two of the clock till three. So I came to see what these objects were."

It was not a volcano after all, not even a lion. The rumbling noise was Miss Andrew snoring.

"The fruit is from Jane and me," Michael told him, "and the chocolate from Mary Poppins."

"Mary Poppins?" Luti murmured the name to himself as though he were remembering something that he had long forgotten.

"There she is." Michael nodded to where Mary Poppins stood by the pear tree, rocking Annabel in the perambulator.

"Peace and blessings to her," said Luti,

waving his hand at the upright figure with the large pink rose in its hat. "I will hide these gifts within my pockets and eat them at night when I go to bed. Missanda eats only porridge."

"Is it a nice bed?" Jane enquired. She wanted to hear about everything that happened in Number Eighteen.

"Well, perhaps it is a little soft. On my island we do not sleep in beds but on mats that my mother weaves for us from the leaves of the coconut palm."

"You could lie on the floor," said Michael. "That would be almost as good."

"No, I must do as Missanda wishes. I am here to be of comfort to her, measure her many medicines, cook the porridge when the fire is hot and study my seven-times-seven. That my parents promised her, for they think she is a learned person and will send me some day back to the island with knowledge of many things."

"But aren't you lonely?" Jane asked him. "And aren't they lonely for you?"

She was thinking how she herself would feel if Miss Andrew took her far away and of how her parents would grieve. No, no such thing could ever happen, not for all the knowledge in the world.

Luti's face crumpled. The smile faded.

"I am lonely forever," his voice was husky. "But a promise has been made to her. If they have need of me, they will send –"

"A telegram!" exclaimed Michael. "In a yellow envelope." A telegram was always exciting.

"On the island we have no such things. But my grandmother, Keria, said for my comfort, 'When we have need of you, it will be known.' She is a Wise Woman. She reads the stars and understands what the sea is saying. But, harken! I hear the bells singing!"

Luti put his hand to his ear as the church clock beyond the Park rang out. "One, Two, Three!" it said. And at the same moment the rumbling from Number Eighteen stopped, as though switched off.

"Missanda has woken from her sleep." Luti hurriedly gathered up fruit and chocolate and stuffed them into his pockets.

"Peace and blessings!" He raised his hand, his bright glance taking in Mary Poppins as well as Jane and Michael.

Then he turned and ran across the lawn, his feet in Mr Banks' big boots crushing the grass as he went.

A door opened and closed behind him and Number Eighteen, suddenly, was as soundless as it had always been.

But the next day, and all the days after it, promptly at two o'clock, the rumbling began again.

"Preposterous! Not to be borne! We must complain to the Prime Minister!" said the people in the Lane. But they knew that even the Prime Minister could no more stop somebody snoring than he could say "Halt!" to a snow-storm. They would just have to grin and bear it.

So that was what they did. And the grinning and bearing made them realise that Miss Andrew's snoring had its fortunate side. For now, between two and three o'clock, they could meet the smiling brown-faced stranger she had brought from the other side of the world. Otherwise, they would never have seen him, cooped up as he was, like a bird in a cage.

So, as well as the fruit that Jane and Michael put on the fence every afternoon – Mary Poppins always in the background – Luti soon found himself showered with gifts.

Mrs Nineteen gave him a paper fan, such as she would like to have made for the grandmother she had never known.

Mr Twenty, a gruff, shy man, presented him with the King and Queen of an old chess set from his attic.

Admiral Boom, in a voice that would have roused from sleep anyone but Miss Andrew, hailed him with "Ahoy there, shipmate!" and pressed upon him a six-inch-long carved canoe, faded and shiny from spending years in the dark of a trouser pocket. "It's my mascot!" He explained. "Brought me luck all my life, ever since I was a midshipman sailing the South Seas."

Binnacle, the retired pirate, gave him a

dagger with a broken point. "It's me second-best," he apologized, "but it'll slit a throat or two if you're minded to become a pirate."

Luti had no desire to become a pirate, far less to slit anyone's throat, but he took the dagger with gratitude and hid it carefully inside his jacket in case Miss Andrew should see it.

The Park Keeper, too, had a present for him – a page out of an exercise book on which he had printed in large letters, "Observe the Rules. Remember the Bye-laws".

"You'll need this," he said earnestly, "if you ever get to come to the Park."

Luti spelled out the strange words. "What is a Bye-law?" he wanted to know.

The Park Keeper scratched his head. "I don't rightly know myself, but it's something you have to remember."

To remember something he did not know! This seemed like a riddle to Luti. But he put the paper into his pocket and decided to think about it.

Even Andrew and Willoughby from Number Sixteen, came each with a bone in his mouth.

And when Luti opened the gate they deposited the bones before him, and walked home waving their tails proudly and feeling noble and generous.

"Peace and blessings!" said Luti, smiling — which was what he said to everyone — and hid the bones under the hedge so that some day another dog would find them.

Everyone wanted to know him. If they had lost Number Eighteen, they had been given a sun-browned stranger who for one hour, every day, smiled upon them and blessed them.

But the stolen hour was mostly spent with Jane and Michael at the hole in the fence, which seemed to be no longer a hole but a place where North and South met, and roses and columbines took the air with waving coconut palms.

Jane and Michael shared their toys, and taught Luti to play Ludo, while he made them whistles from leaves of grass, told them about the coral island and stories of his ancestors who came from the Land of the Sun. And of his grandmother, Keria, who knew the language of birds and beasts and how to subdue a thunderstorm.

Jane and Michael many times wished they had a
Wise Woman for a grandmother. Aunt Flossie
would never be able to deal with thunder. All
she could do was escape from it by getting under
a bed.

And always, as if by chance – but they knew
that nothing she did was by chance – Mary
Poppins would be at hand, rocking Annabel to
sleep, playing with John and Barbara, or sitting
on the garden seat reading *Everything a Lady
Should Know*.

But there came a day when the clock struck two
and Jane and Michael went to the hole to find no
Luti there.

It was Monday, and therefore Washing Day.
It was also dim and misty as though a cloud had
swallowed the sun.

"Just my luck!" said Mrs Brill, as she
pegged the sheets on the lines. "I need the sun,
but it doesn't need me."

The mist did not bother Jane and Michael.
They merely waited, peering through it, for a

glimpse of a well-known figure. But when at last it did come, it was not the Luti they knew. He was bent and huddled like an old, old man, with his arms hugging his chest. And as he threw himself down beside them, they saw that he was weeping.

"What is it, Luti? We have brought you some pears. Don't you want to eat them?"

"No, no, I am troubled in my heart. Something is trying to speak to me. I can hear a knocking."

"Where?" They looked about uneasily. There was no sound anywhere but the rise and fall of Miss Andrew's snoring.

"In here." Luti beat his breast, rocking himself to and fro. "They are calling to me – knock, knock, knock! Keria said I would surely know. They are telling me to come home. Alas, what must I do?" He looked at the children, with streaming eyes. "The lady with the flower in her hat – she would understand."

"Mary Poppins!" Michael shouted. "Mary Poppins, where are you?"

"I am not deaf, nor in Timbuctoo. And you,

Michael, are not a hyena. Kindly speak more quietly. Annabel is asleep."

The hat with the pink rose bobbing on it leaned over the top of the fence. "Tell me, what is the matter, Luti?" Mary Poppins looked down at the sobbing child.

"I hear a knocking inside me, here." Luti put his hand on his heart. "I think they are sending for me."

"Then the moment has come for you to go home. Climb through the hole and follow me."

"But Missanda – her porridge, her medicines, and my learning of many things!" Luti eyed her anxiously.

"Miss Andrew will be taken care of," said Mary Poppins, firmly. "Come with me, all of you. There is not much time."

Jane and Michael helped the half-unwilling boy hurriedly through the gap. And Mary Poppins took his hand, placing it closely beside her own on the handle of the perambulator, as the little procession made its way through a corridor of wet white sheets.

They were all silent as they hurried through

the misty garden, across the Lane where the ripe
cherries hung from the branches, each cluster
veiled in white, and into the Park with its hazy
shapes of bushes, trees and swings.

The Park Keeper, like an eager dog, came
lolloping towards them. "Observe the Rules.
Remember the Bye-laws! You've got it on your
piece of paper," he said, looking at Luti.

"Observe them yourself," said Mary
Poppins. "There's some wastepaper over
there. Put it in the litter bin."

The Park Keeper turned sulkily away and
went towards the litter. "Who does she think
she is?" he muttered. But no answer came to
his question.

Mary Poppins marched on, stopping only at
the edge of the Lake to admire her own reflection, with its misty rose-bedecked hat and the
wide knitted scarf with its matching roses that
today she wore round her shoulders.

"Where are we going, Mary Poppins?"
Where *could* they go in the mist, thought Jane.

"Walk up, walk up!" said Mary Poppins.
And it seemed to the children that she was herself

55

walking up, putting her foot upon the cloud as if it were a staircase and tilting up the perambulator as though climbing a hill.

And suddenly, they were all climbing, leaving the Park behind them, walking upon the misty substance that seemed as firm as a snow-drift. Luti leaned against Mary Poppins as though she were the one safe thing in the world, and together they pushed the perambulator while Jane and Michael followed.

"Observe the Rules!" the Park Keeper shouted. "You can't climb the clouds. It's against the Bye-laws! I shall have to inform the Prime Minister."

"Do!" Mary Poppins called over her shoulder, as she led them higher and higher.

On they went, ever upwards, with the mist growing firmer at every step and the sky around them brighter. Till at last, as though they had come to the top of a staircase, a gleaming cloud-field spread out before them as flat and white as a plate. The sun lay across it in stripes of gold and, to the children's astonishment, a huge full moon confronted them, anchored, as it were, at the edge of a cloud.

It was crowded with objects of every description – umbrellas, handbags, books, toys, luggage, parcels, cricket bats, caps, coats, slippers, gloves, the kind of things people leave behind them in buses or trains or on seats in a park.

And among these varied articles, with a small iron cooking stove beside it, stood an old battered armchair, and in the chair sat a bald-headed man in the act of raising a cup to his lips.

"Uncle! Stop! Don't you dare drink it!" Mary Poppins' voice rang out sharply and the cup banged down into its saucer.

"What, what? Who? Where?" With a start, the man lifted his head. "Oh, it's you, Mary! You gave me a fright. I was just going to take a sip of cocoa."

"You were, indeed, and you know quite well that cocoa makes one sleepy!" She leaned in and took the cup from his hand.

"It's not fair," grumbled the uncle. "Everyone else can indulge themselves with a soothing drink. But not me, not the poor Man-in-the-Moon. He has to stay awake night and day to keep a watch on things. And anyway, people should be more careful and not go losing tins of cocoa – yes, and cups to put the cocoa in."

"That's our cup!" Michael exclaimed. "Mrs Brill said when she broke it that it would be needed somewhere else."

"Well, it was. So I glued the bits together. And then someone dropped a tin of cocoa" – he glanced at the tin on the edge of the stove and Jane remembered that such a one had fallen from the string bag on their way home from the grocer's.

"And I had a packet of sugar by me, so you see, with three such treats coming together, I just couldn't resist them. I'm sorry, Mary. I won't do it again, I promise." The Man-in-the-Moon looked shamefaced.

"You won't get the chance," said Mary Poppins, seizing the tin from the top of the stove and stuffing it into her handbag.

"Well, goodbye cocoa, goodbye sleep!" The Man-in-the-Moon sighed heavily. Then he grinned and looked at Jane and Michael. "Did you ever know anyone like her?" he asked.

"Never, never!" they both replied.

"Of course you didn't," he beamed proudly. "She's the One and Only."

"Do all lost things come to the Moon?" Jane thought of the lost things in the world and wondered if there was room for them.

"Mostly, yes," said the Man-in-the-Moon. "It's a kind of storehouse."

"And what's at the back of it?" asked Michael. "We only see this side."

"Ah, if I knew that, I'd know a lot. It's a mystery, a kind of riddle – a front without a back you might say, as far as I'm concerned. Besides, it's very overcrowded. You couldn't relieve me of anything, could you? Something you might have lost in the Park?"

"I can!" said Jane, suddenly, for among the parcels and umbrellas she had spied a shabby, familiar shape.

"The Blue Duck!" She reached for the faded toy. "The Twins dropped it out of the

perambulator."

"And there's my dear old mouth organ." Michael pointed to a metal shape on the shelf above the stove. "But it doesn't make music any more. It's really no use to me."

"Nor to me, either. I have tried it. A musical instrument that can't make music! Take it, there's a good fellow, and put it in your pocket."

Michael reached for the mouth organ and as he did so, something that was lying beside it toppled sideways and came bouncing down, rolling out over the cloud.

"Oh, that is mine, my lost coconut!" Luti stepped out from behind Mary Poppins and seized the moving object. It was brown and shaggy, round as a ball, one side of it closely shaven with a round face carved upon it.

Luti hugged the hairy thing to his breast.

"My father carved it," he said, proudly, "and I lost it one day in the tide of the sea."

"And now the tide has given it back. But you, young man, should be on your way. They are all waiting for you on the island and Keria is at her clay stove making spells with herbs for your safe return. Your father has lately hurt his arm and he needs your help in the canoe." The Man-in-the-Moon spoke firmly to Luti.

"He *is* on his way," said Mary Poppins. "That is why we are here."

"Ha! I knew you had something up your sleeve. You never visit me, Mary, my dear, just for a friendly cup of tea – or perhaps I should say cocoa!" The Man-in-the-Moon grinned impishly.

"I want you to keep an eye on him. He is young for such a long journey, uncle."

"As if I could help it – you know that. Not a wink will I take, much less forty! Trust your old uncle, my girl."

"How do you know Keria?" asked Jane. The thought of the Wise Woman far away filled her with a kind of dream. She wished she could know her, too.

"In the same way that I know everyone. It's my job to watch and wake. The world turns and I turn with the world; mountain and sea, city and desert; the leaf on the bough and the bough bare; men sleeping, waking, working; the cradle child, the old woman, the wise ones and the not so wise; you in your smock, Michael in his sailor blouse; the children on Luti's South Sea island in their girdles of leaves and wreaths of flowers such as he, too, will wear in the morning. Those things he has on now, Mary, would be most unsuitable."

"I have thought of that, thank you," said Mary Poppins, unfastening Luti's stiff collar and, with her usual lightning speed, sweeping off jacket and knickerbockers and Mr Banks' big boots. Then, as he stood there in his underwear, she wound about him, as one would a parcel, her knitted scarf with its pink roses that matched the one on her hat.

"But my treasures! I must take them with me." Luti eyed her earnestly.

Mary Poppins took from the perambulator a battered paper bag. "Fuss, fuss, fuss!" she said, with a sniff, as he fished in the pockets of his jacket.

"I could take care of the dagger for you." Michael was secretly envious. He had often had thoughts of becoming a pirate.

"One must never give away a gift. My father will use it for his carving and cutting twigs for the fire."

Luti stuffed the dagger into his bag with the fan, the wooden King and Queen and the Admiral's canoe. Last of all came a dark and sticky lump of something wrapped up in a handkerchief.

"The chocolate bar!" Jane exclaimed. "We thought you had eaten it up."

"It was too precious," said Luti, simply. "We have no such sweetmeats on the island. They shall have a taste of it, all of them."

He reached an arm out of the scarf and stowed the bag in its woollen folds. Then he picked up the shaggy coconut, held it for a moment to his heart, before thrusting it at the children.

"Remember me, please," he said shyly. "I am indeed sad to leave you."

Mary Poppins picked up the folded clothes and laid them neatly on the floor of the moon.

"Come, Luti, it is time to go. I will show you the way. Jane and Michael, take care of the little ones. Uncle, remember your promise."

She put her arm round the pink knitted bundle and Luti turned within it, smiling.

"Peace and blessings!" He held up his hand.

"Peace and blessings!" cried Jane and Michael.

"Do exactly as she tells you," said the Man-in-the-Moon, "and Peace and blessings, my boy!"

They watched him being marched away over the white cloudy field to the place where it met the sky. There Mary Poppins bent down to him, pointing to a string of cloudlets that floated like puffballs in the blue. They saw Luti nod as he gazed at them, saw him hold up his hand in a farewell gesture, then his bare legs took a little run that ended in an enormous leap.

"Oh Luti!" they cried anxiously, and gasped with relief as he landed safely in the middle of the nearest puffball. Then he was skimming lightly across it and jumping onto the next. On, on he went, bounding over the gulfs of air between the floating clouds.

A shrill sound came back to them. He was singing, they could distinguish the words:

"I am Luti, Son of the Sun,
I am wearing a garment of roses,
I am going home to my island,
Peace and blessings, O clouds!"

Then he was silent and lost to sight. Mary Poppins was standing beside them and the moon, when they turned to look at it, was off on its course, sailing away.

"Goodbye!" called Jane and Michael, waving. And the faint shape of an arm waved back with an answering call of "Au Revoir!".

Mary Poppins brandished her parrot-headed umbrella and then turned to the children. "Now, quick march and best foot forward!"

The pink rose bobbed jauntily on her hat as she gave the perambulator a twist and sent it rolling on a downward slope.

They seemed to be sliding rather than walking with the cloud growing mistier every second. Soon the shapes of trees loomed through the haze and suddenly, instead of air, there was solid earth beneath their feet and the Park Keeper and the Prime Minister were coming towards them, on the Long Walk, the emerging sun bright on their faces.

"There they are, just like I told you, coming right down out of the sky, breaking the Rules and the Bye-laws!"

"Nonsense, Smith, they had merely walked into the mist and now that it's lifted you can see them again. It has nothing to do with the Bye-laws. Good afternoon, Miss Mary Poppins. I must apologize for the Park Keeper. One would think, to hear him talk, that you had been visiting the Moon, ha, ha!"

The Prime Minister laughed at his own joke.

"One would indeed!" Mary Poppins replied, with a gracious, innocent smile.

"And what have you done with the other one?" the Park Keeper demanded. "The little brown fellow – left him up in the air?" He had seen Luti with the family troupe and now he was with it no longer.

The Prime Minister regarded him sternly. "Really, Smith, you go too far. How could anyone be left in the sky, supposing he could get there? You see, as we all do, shapes in the mist and your imagination runs away with you. Get on with your work in the Park, my man, and don't go molesting innocent people who are simply strolling through it. But now I must run away myself. They say there is trouble in the Lane. Someone appears to have lost their wits and I must look into it, I suppose. Good-day to you, Miss Mary Poppins. Next time you go climbing into the blue, pray give my respects to the Man-in-the-Moon!''

And, again laughing heartily, the Prime Minister swept off his hat and hurried away through the Park Gates.

Mary Poppins smiled to herself as she and the children followed closely behind him.

Angrily staring after them, the Park Keeper stood in the Long Walk. She had made a fool of him again! He was sure she had been up in the sky and he wished with all his heart she had stayed there.

There was, indeed, trouble in the Lane.

70

A large woman, with a big black bag in one hand, and tearing her hair with the other, was standing at the gate of Number Eighteen, alternately shouting and sobbing.

And Miss Lark's dogs, usually so quiet, were jumping up and down, barking at her.

Of course it was Miss Andrew.

Mary Poppins, cautiously walking on tiptoe, signalled to the children to do the same as they followed in the steps of the Prime Minister.

He was clearly nervous when he reached the scene.

"Er – is there anything, Madam, I can do to help you?"

Miss Andrew seized him by the arm. "Have you seen Luti?" she demanded. "Luti has gone. I have lost Luti. Oh, oh, oh!"

"Well," the Prime Minister glanced around anxiously. "I am not quite sure what a Luti is." It might, he thought, be a dog, or a cat, even, perhaps a parrot. "If I knew, I could, perhaps, be of use."

"He looks after me and measures my medicines and gives them to me at the proper times."

"Oh, a chemist! No, I have seen no chemist. Certainly not a lost one."

"And he makes my porridge in the morning."

"A cook, then. No, I have not seen a cook."

"He comes from the South Seas and I've lost him!" Miss Andrew burst anew into sobs.

The Prime Minister looked astonished. A cook – or a chemist – from the South Seas! Such a one, if lost, would be hard to find.

"Well, give me your bag and we'll take a walk along the Lane. Somebody may have seen him. You, perhaps, madam," he said to Miss Lark, who was hurrying in pursuit of her dogs.

"No!" said Miss Lark. "Neither have Andrew and Willoughby!" She was not going to have anything to do with the woman whose snoring had disturbed the Lane.

The two dogs followed her, angrily growling. And the Prime Minister urged Miss Andrew along, letting her keep her grasp on his arm, as they went from gate to gate.

No, Mrs Nineteen had seen nothing. That was all she would say. And Mr Twenty repeated her words. Neither felt sympathy for Miss

73

Andrew. She had taken their precious Number Eighteen and, moreover, had kept locked up within it, the sunny stranger who, for just one little hour a day, they had come to love and respect. If Luti were indeed lost they hoped that some better fate would find him.

"No, no, always no! Will nobody help me?" wailed Miss Andrew, grasping the Prime Minister more tightly.

And behind them, like a soundless shadow, the perambulator swept along, with Mary Poppins and Jane and Michael walking softly on the grass.

The Prime Minister's arm was beginning to ache as Miss Andrew, continually lamenting, drew him towards Binnacle's ship-shaped cottage which stood at the end of the Lane.

Binacle was sitting on his front doorstep, playing his concertina and the Admiral, with Mrs Boom beside him, was singing at the top of his voice his favourite sea-shanty.

"Sailing, sailing, over the bounding main,
And many a stormy wind shall blow
Till Jack comes home again."

74

"Stop! Stop!" Miss Andrew shrieked. "Listen to what I have to tell you. Luti is lost. He has gone away."

The Admiral broke off in mid-song. The concertina was silent.

"Blast my gizzard! Lost, you say? I don't believe it – he's a sensible lad. He's probably simply up-anchored and gone to join the navy. That's what a sensible lad would do. Don't you think so, Prime Minister?"

Privately, the Prime Minister did not think so at all. The navy, he felt, had all the cooks and chemists it needed. But he knew from experience that if he disagreed with the Admiral he would be advised to go to sea and he preferred being a landlubber.

"Well, perhaps," he said uneasily, "we must enquire further."

"But what shall I do?" Miss Andrew broke in. "He's lost and I've nowhere to go!"

"You've Number Eighteen," Mrs Boom said, gently. "Isn't that enough?"

"Ask Binnacle!" said Admiral Boom. "He has an extra cabin. Plenty of room for her and her chattels."

Binnacle glanced at the Admiral. Then he eyed Miss Andrew reflectively. "Well, I could manage the medicines and all pirates know how to cook porridge. But . . ." his voice now held a note of warning, ". . . you've got to pay the price!"

Relief dawned on Miss Andrew's face. "Oh, anything! Ask any price you like. I will gladly pay it." She loosened her grasp on the Prime Minister's arm.

"Nah, nah, it's not the money. *You* need someone to cook and measure and *I* need someone to read to me – not once or twice but whenever I'm free!"

"Oh, I could think of nothing better." A smile made its way onto Miss Andrew's face which was not used to smiling. "I have many books I could bring with me and teach you what I taught Luti."

"Look, lady. I don't want no 'eddication'. All a pirate needs to learn is how to be a pirate. But . . ." and again there was a note of warning, ". . . I won't have anyone in my house unless they can be a proper shipmate and dance the Sailor's Hornpipe!"

"The Hornpipe!" Miss Andrew was shocked. "I could never think of such a thing. Besides, I don't even know it!"

"Of course you could!" said the Admiral. "Everyone on sea or land can do the Sailor's Hornpipe. All you need is to hear the music. Strike a chord, Binnacle. Up with the anchor!"

Binnacle grinned at the Admiral, and the concertina, at a touch of his hand, broke into the rocking tune.

The Admiral's feet began to twitch, so did Mrs Boom's. So did the Prime Minister's. And Mrs Nineteen and Mr Twenty, hearing the sound from their front gardens, began to sway with the music.

But Miss Andrew stood as if carved in stone, her face fierce and determined. 'Nothing will move me,' it seemed to say, 'not even an earthquake'.

Mary Poppins regarded her thoughtfully, as the music grew wilder and wilder. Then she plucked the mouth organ from Michael's pocket and put it to her lips.

Immediately a tune broke from it keeping time with the concertina. And slowly, slowly, as though against its will, the stone figure thrust from beneath its skirts two large feet that had never danced but were now begining to shuffle. Heel and toe, away we go, across the bounding main.

And suddenly they were all sailors, Miss Andrew among them, unwillingly moving her great bulk through the measures of the hornpipe.

The Twins and Annabel bobbed up and down. Jane and Michael pranced beside them, while the cherry trees bent and bowed and the cherries twirled on their stems. Only Mary Poppins stood still, the mouth organ, held against her lips, giving out its lively tune.

Then it was over, the last chord played, and everyone – except Miss Andrew – was breathless and pleased with themselves.

"Bravo, messmate!" the Admiral roared, doffing his hat to the stony figure.

But the stony figure took no notice. It had caught sight suddenly of Mary Poppins, stuffing

the mouth organ into Michael's pocket.

A long, long look, as of two wolves meeting, passed between the pair.

"You again!" Miss Andrew's face was contorted with rage and the realization that for the second time Mary Poppins had bamboozled her. "It was you who made me perform like that – so shameful, so undignified! And you, You, YOU, who sent Luti away!" She pointed a large, trembling finger at the calm and smiling figure.

"Nonsense, madam, you are much mistaken," the Prime Minister broke in. "No one can force another to dance. You owe it to your own two feet, and very apt they were. As for Miss Poppins, a respectable well-behaved young woman, always so busy with her charges, could such a one gallivant about, dispatching cooks – or for that matter, chemists – to somewhere in the South Seas? Certainly not. It's unthinkable!"

Jane and Michael looked at each other. The unthinkable, they knew, had been thought. It had, indeed, recently happened. And Luti was on his way to his homeland.

"Everyone needs his own home," said Mary Poppins calmly. And she twirled the perambulator round and sent it speeding homewards.

"And I need mine," cried Miss Andrew wildly, flinging herself against Binnacle's front door.

"Well, you've got one here," said Binnacle. "Unless . . ." he smiled a terrible pirate smile, ". . . unless you'd prefer Number Eighteen."

"Oh, never, never! Not without Luti!" Miss Andrew buried her face in her hands. And before she knew it, Binnacle and the Prime Minister – who was still holding the Medicine bag – had hustled her into the house.

"Well, she's safely in port," said Admiral Boom. "They'll put her on an even keel."

And, taking Mrs Boom's arm, he allowed her to lead him away.

It was growing dark when Mr Banks, coming along the Lane, glanced at Binnacle's front window and beheld a curious sight. In a small room, clean and bare as the deck of a ship, sat Miss Andrew in the only chair, looking like somebody who has been shipwrecked. An empty glass stood on a table nearby and beside her, squatting on his haunches, was Binnacle, absorbed in something she was reading aloud – an activity that, from the look on her face, filled her with rage and disgust.

And, in the doorway, intently listening, was no less a person than the Prime Minister. The Head of the State in Cherry Tree Lane concerning himself with the goings-on in the home of an ex-pirate!

Amazed, Mr Banks took off his hat. "Can I be of service, Prime Minister? Is anything amiss?"

"Oh, Banks, my dear fellow, such tribulations! The lady whom you see inside has vacated Number Eighteen because her companion – a cook or a chemist, I'm not sure which – has apparently deserted her. And Binnacle, the Admiral's servant, has taken her to live with him on two important conditions – one, that she dance the Sailor's Hornpipe and the other, that she read to him. Well, she has danced, though unwillingly, and now she is reading aloud."

"I am flabbergasted!" said Mr Banks. "Miss Andrew dancing! Luti gone! I think you should know, Prime Minister, that that companion was neither a cook nor a chemist but a boy hardly taller than my daughter Jane, who was brought by Miss Andrew from the Southern Seas."

"A child! Good Heavens, we must get the police! A lost boy must be searched for."

"I wouldn't advise it, Prime Minister. The police might frighten him. Give him just a little more time. He's a bright lad. He will find his way."

"We-ell, if you think so. You know them better than I."

"I do, indeed. Miss Andrew was once my governess. And she's known as the Holy Terror. The boy has had a lucky escape."

"Ha! Well, it's Binnacle now who's the Holy Terror. He has given her cold porridge to eat, made her drink various medicines mixed together in a single glass, and he won't let her read to him anything but copies – new or old – of *Fizzo!*"

"*Fizzo!* But that's a comic, surely. And Miss Andrew is a learned woman. Having to read comics aloud will simply horrify her. Perhaps it will even drive her mad."

"Well, I happen to like them, Banks. I get so weary of making laws that I find *Fizzo* quite restful. We have just had *Tiger Tim and the Tortoise* and are now in the middle of *Sam's Adventure*. So, excuse me, please, my dear fellow. I must hear how he and Gwendolyn manage to deal with the Dragon."

"Oh, of course!" said Mr Banks, politely.

And, leaving the Prime Minister craning his head to catch the story, he hurried home full of the evening's news.

Number Eighteen, as he passed it, had something of its old friendly look and Miss Lark's dogs were busily sniffing at something under the hedge. They could smell the old bones they had given Luti and, since he seemed to have gone away, they were anxious to retrieve them. Why leave such treasures for other dogs?

84

"I have news for you," Mr Banks exclaimed, as Mrs Banks met him at the door. "The sensation of the year, my dear! Luti is no longer with us and Miss Andrew has left Next Door and gone to live with Binacle."

Mrs Banks gave an astonished shriek and collapsed upon a chair.

"Luti lost? Oh, that poor dear child! Shouldn't we go and look for him? So young and in a strange land."

"Oh, Luti has a good head on his shoulders. He's probably made his way to the docks and stowed away on some trading ship. It's Miss Andrew I'm thinking about. She kept that boy like a bird in a cage and now she's a bird in a cage herself, reading stories from *Fizzo*."

"*Fizzo*? Miss Andrew? I can't believe it." It was Mrs Banks' turn to be flabbergasted.

Mr Banks was almost dancing with joy. He was thinking that now his astronomer would soon be in his old haunts again, his telescope turned to the sky. He did not yet know that all Next Door's invisible dwellers were already back in their places – the grandmother, the chess companions, Admiral Boom's brave sea captain, Mrs Boom's quiet child, Mrs Banks' friendly friend, the Sleeping Beauty, Gobbo. Nor did he realise that even the nettles had begun to sprout in the garden again.

"Think of it!" he cried with delight. "Number Eighteen empty again and with luck we'll keep it so!"

"But, George, shouldn't we think of Miss Andrew? Will she be able to endure such a life?"

"No, my dear, I'm sure she won't. It's my belief that Binnacle will wake up one morning and find himself deserted – no one to read aloud to him. Miss Andrew, as we know, has a mind of her own. She's a learned woman and a born teacher. And teachers have to teach. She'll skip off somewhere, I'll be bound. Last time it was to the South. Perhaps she'll make her way Northwards and find an Eskimo, heaven help him! You mark my words, the Lane will have seen the last of her sooner than you think."

"Well, I hope so," murmured Mrs Banks. "We have had enough of that terrible snoring. Michael!" She broke off at the sight of a figure in pyjamas perched on the banisters. "You ought to be in bed!"

"And what do you think you're doing?" asked his father. "Trying to climb up the banisters?"

"I'm being a pirate," Michael panted, attempting to pull himself higher.

"Well, no one, not even a pirate, can climb *up* banisters. It's against the laws of nature. And by the way – I'm sorry to have to tell you this – Luti has gone away. We won't be seeing him again, I'm afraid."

"I know," said Michael – knowing too, though he did not say so, that Someone *had* climbed the banisters. Someone, in fact, who was not far away.

"Really!" said Mr Banks testily. "I can't think how it so often happens that my children seem to know what's afoot before I get a hint of it. Be off with you, on your two feet, like any civilized being."

Michael went unwillingly. He did not like being civilized.

At the top of the stairs Mary Poppins was

waiting, a blue-clad statue with an arm out-
stretched that pointed to his bed.

"Oh, not again, please, Mary Poppins. I'm
tired of going to bed every night."

"The night is for sleeping," she said, primly.
"So, in with you, spit-spot. And you, too, if
you please, Jane."

For Jane, holding Luti's coconut, was kneel-
ing on the window seat watching the full moon
sailing the sky low down on the horizon. There
was somebody there, though she could not see
him, for whom no night was for sleeping.

"And I'll take care of that. Thank you!"
Mary Poppins took the coconut and glanced at
the carved smiling face that seemed to repeat,
though wordlessly, Luti's phrase of, "Peace and
blessings!".

She placed it on the mantelpiece and as she
did so her image looked at her from the mirror
and the two exchanged a nod of approval.

"But I wanted to watch and wake,"
grumbled Michael.

To his surprise Mary Poppins said nothing.
She merely placed a chair by his bed and with a

wide dramatic gesture invited him to sit down.

He did so, full of determination. He, too, would see Luti on his way.

But soon his eyes began to close. He propped them open with his fingers. But then he yawned, an enormous yawn, that seemed to swallow him up.

"I'd better do it tomorrow," he said, and rolled sideways into the bed that Mary Poppins, with a look that said more than words, was turning down for him.

"Tomorrow never comes," said Jane. "When you wake up it's always today." And she too climbed into bed.

They lay there, watching Mary Poppins making her usual whirlwind round, tucking in Annabel and the Twins, pushing the rocking horse into his corner, taking things out of pockets, folding up the clothes. As she came to Michael's sailor blouse, she tossed the mouth organ to him.

He decided to give it another try, blowing in and blowing out, but again the mouth organ was silent.

"It still won't work for me," he said, "and it wouldn't for the Man-in-the-Moon. I wonder, Mary Poppins, why it worked for you when you played the Sailor's Hornpipe?"

She favoured him with a quick blue glance. "I wonder!" she said, mockingly, and went on being a whirlwind.

Jane too, would have liked to watch and wake, but she knew that she could not do it. So she lay still, thinking of Luti – picturing the singing, leaping figure, wrapped in the scarf of woollen roses, careering across the sky. For Luti, too, the night was not for sleeping. And suddenly, she was anxious.

"Suppose, Mary Poppins," she burst out. "Suppose there are not enough clouds up there to take him all the way!" She remembered many a clear, bright night when from corner to corner of the world, there was nothing but dark blue sky. "What if he came to an empty space? How could he go further?"

"There's always a cloud about somewhere," said Mary Poppins, comfortably. And she set a match to the wick of the nightlight where it stood

on the mantelpiece, a small and glowing like-
ness of the big lamp on the table. As usual, it
would watch all night. And the two lamps filled
the room with shadows that were themselves like
clouds.

Jane felt reassured. "When the morning
comes he will be at home, under the coconut
palms. And we, too, will be at home, but under
the cherry trees. It's different, but somehow the
same."

"East. West. Home's Best," said Mary Poppins, cheerfully, as she hung the parrot-
headed umbrella on its accustomed hook.

"And you, Mary Poppins," Jane demanded,
knowing that it was a daring question. "Where
is your home – East or West? Where do you go
when you're not here?"

"Everyone needs his own home – that's what
you said today, remember?" Michael, too, was
daring.

Mary Poppins stood by the table, a whirlwind
no longer, her day's work over.

The glow from the big lamp lit up her face, the
pink cheeks, the blue eyes, the turned-up nose.

She looked at them both reflectively while they waited, hardly breathing. Where did she come from – woodland or field, cottage or castle, mountain or sea? Would she or wouldn't she tell them?

"Oh, she would!" they thought, for her face was so vivid, so brimful of things that remained to be told.

Then a sparkle leapt to the blue eyes and the old, familiar, secret smile greeted their eager faces.

"I'm at home," she said, "wherever I am!"

And with that, she turned out the lamp.

A.M.G.D.